THE TRAVELING PEN

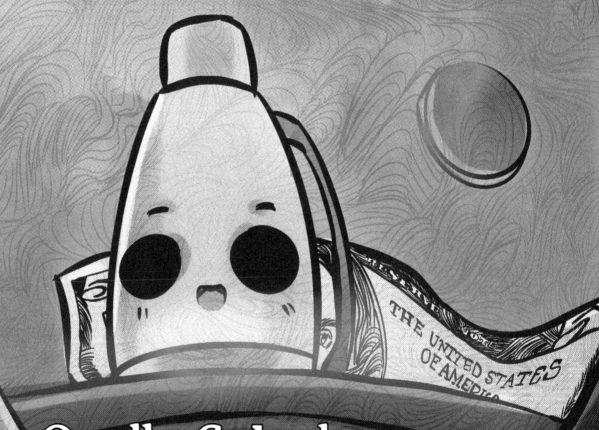

THE TRAVELING PEN

MY NEW HOME

Quella C. Jackson

XULON PRESS

Xulon Press
2301 Lucien Way #415
Maitland, FL 32751
407.339.4217
www.xulonpress.com

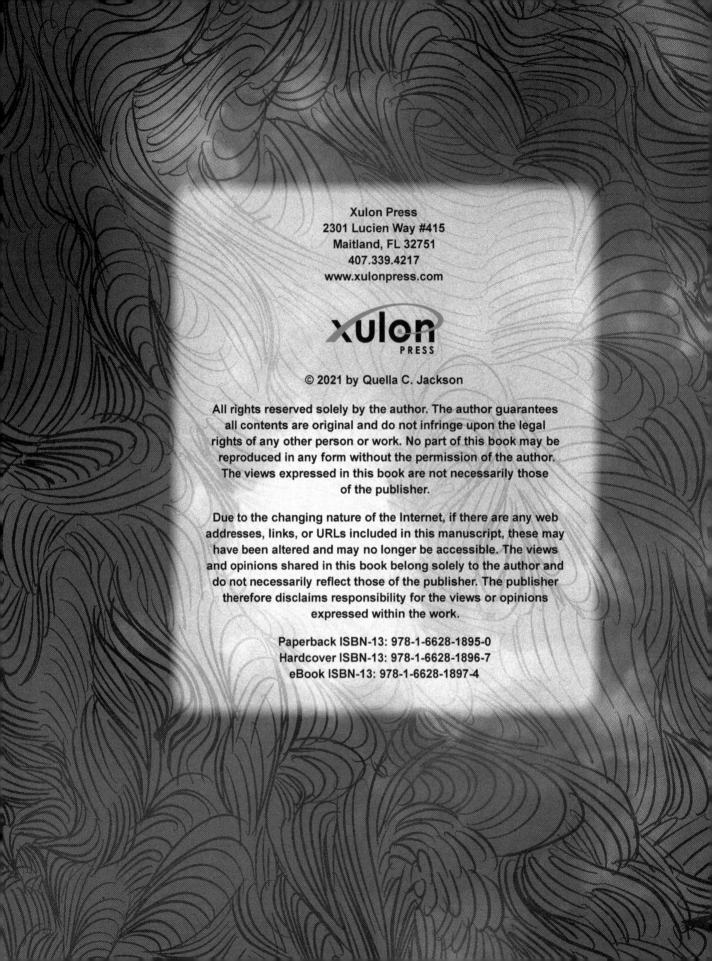

Paperback ISBN-13: 978-1-6628-1895-0
Hardcover ISBN-13: 978-1-6628-1896-7
eBook ISBN-13: 978-1-6628-1897-4

This book is dedicated to all the children who are or have been in the foster care system. Whether you are in a foster home, a group home, a treatment center, or an adoptive home, God is always with you.

Boligrafo was a young ink pen who belonged to a human named Ms. Flora. She wore a cheerful, pink suit that shined like the sun on a Sunday afternoon. Ms. Flora had an inspiring love for traveling and cherished writing down her memories of her trips. She treasured Boligrafo and took him everywhere she went. Although Boligrafo was still young, he took delight in the places Ms. Flora utilized him to write about.

2

Sometimes Ms. Flora would panic if she could not find Boligrafo, and she would take a deep breath in relief when she remembered where she had left him.

That sound was like musical windchimes to Boligrafo's ears. He often heard Ms. Flora say, "You're my favorite pen," and "Oh, this pen writes so well!" Those words made Boligrafo feel appreciated. He was thrilled that he could help her whenever she needed him to. After all, she had given him a safe place to stay.

When Boligrafo asked where he came from, he knew that Ms. Flora could not understand him, but he wondered if anyone around knew anything about his family. He was in luck! Mr. Brown, an old pocketbook, lived at the bottom of Ms. Flora's purse.

He did not get to leave the purse as often as he had in the past, for he was getting older and needed to rest. Over the years, he had made many friends and had learned a lot about those who traveled through.

Mr. Brown heard Boligrafo's question to Ms. Flora.

"Well son, she may not be able to tell you, but I can," said Mr. Brown. "Please, sir, I want to know where I came from."

So, Mr. Brown began to tell the story of how Boligrafo traveled to Ms. Flora's home. Let us all gather around and listen to Boligrafo's story. After all, everyone has a story to tell.

5

Some time ago, there was a family of ten pens who lived together at a local grocery store in their packaged home. Everything seemed to be going well, although there were so many people in that home.

Boligrafo lived with his mom, dad, and big sister, Plumba. His aunt, uncle, and two cousins lived there as well, along with his grandparents.

Boligrafo was just a little ink pen, so he did not remember too much about his family. Sometimes his mom and dad did not get along, and his Uncle Lee Penn would have to help them out by getting them to talk to each other. They would disagree on things like whose turn it was to cook dinner and why the trash had not been taken out.

They would even argue about who put the peanut butter in the refrigerator! It seemed that Momma Penn and Papa Penn were always shouting at one another.

One day, Boligrafo's parents had another argument, but this time, it appeared to be more serious than the others. It seemed like Uncle Lee was not able to help them this time.

Papa Penn was upset because he wanted to use the bill money to buy presents for everyone. Mama Penn did not like that idea, as she felt that paying the bills was the right decision to make. During the argument, Grand Papa Penn stepped in and said, "Stop! Something is not right!"

The house was shaking from all the yelling and screaming, and Grand Momma Penn tried to keep everyone calm as the house continued to shake. The Penns' packaged home shook so much that it fell from the rack in the grocery store and onto the floor. The house hit the ground hard and stayed there until a human stranger walked by.

9

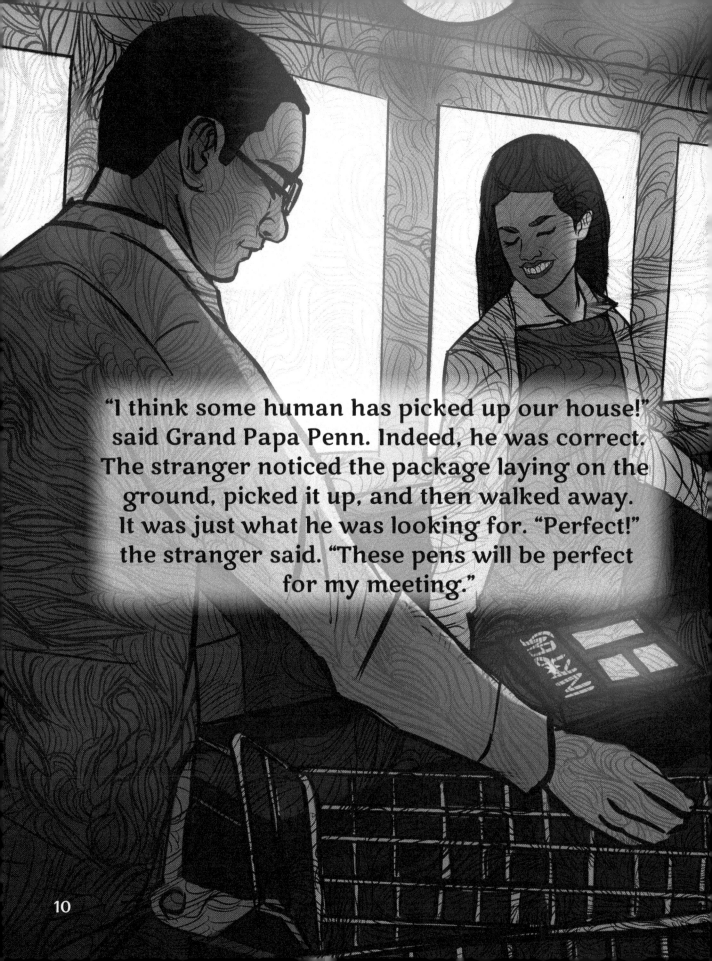

"I think some human has picked up our house!" said Grand Papa Penn. Indeed, he was correct. The stranger noticed the package laying on the ground, picked it up, and then walked away. It was just what he was looking for. "Perfect!" the stranger said. "These pens will be perfect for my meeting."

Boligrafo
interrupted.

"Mr. Brown! How
do you know
all of this?
Are you making
all of this up?"

"I was here when you first arrived in Ms. Flora's purse. You may not remember, but you were nervous and did not talk much to others. Your big sister, Plumba, told us how you both journeyed to your new home here. She stayed with us for a few months until she met Ms. Flora's daughter, Antoinette.

Antoinette needed help with her homework one day, so Plumba was excited to assist. Antoinette is away at college now, and I am sure they are having a great time!"

"Mr. Brown? What happened next? What happened after my house was picked up?" asked Boligrafo.

Mr. Brown continued with Boligrafo's story on how he ended up in his new forever home.

INK PENS

At the grocery store, the stranger examined the package and decided he was going to take it with him to the cash register. The Penns' packaged home was placed in a small, brown shopping bag. From there, the stranger walked out of the store and placed the shopping bag in his car.

The Penn family became afraid and told each other how much they loved one another. Boligrafo's parents apologized to everyone for not getting along.

They felt like this was all their fault and did not know what to do.

The whole household was sad, and Mamma Penn began to weep with grief. The family did not know what was about to happen next, but they knew that life for them would never be the same.

14

Then Grand Mama Penn grew extra quiet and still. Aunt Mary Penn noticed this and asked why she was so quiet.

"Gather around, family. Let us pray," said Grand Mama Penn. "God, please protect my family. Place them in a safe home and bring peace and joy to their lives. In Jesus's name, amen."

Suddenly, the whole family did not feel frightened anymore! They knew that whatever was about to happen, everyone would be okay and safe.

Now, Mr. Brown had been with Ms. Flora for many years. Overtime, while residing in Ms. Flora's purse, he had the pleasure of meeting diverse pens. Ms. Flora did not have to buy pens often because there were plenty of pens to have from her job.

One day, Ms. Flora was in a meeting at work. A gentleman entered the room, swinging a small, brown shopping bag back and forth as he walked. This was the same shopping bag that the Penn family was in. The gentleman placed the bag on a long, wooden table where other people were sitting.

"Hello, everyone! I have some new pens to distribute for our meeting. Feel free to keep as many as you want. I have plenty more," announced the gentleman.

The gentleman then reached his gigantic hand into the brown paper bag, feeling around for the Penn's packaged home. The package of pens shook again, only this time, the gentleman was gripping the package as he pulled it out of the bag. The Penn family looked at each other with sadness, but something told them that everyone would be safe and sound.

The package was ripped open, and it felt like a gush of wind whisked into the Penn's home!
Mama Penn and Papa Penn fell out, landing on the table.

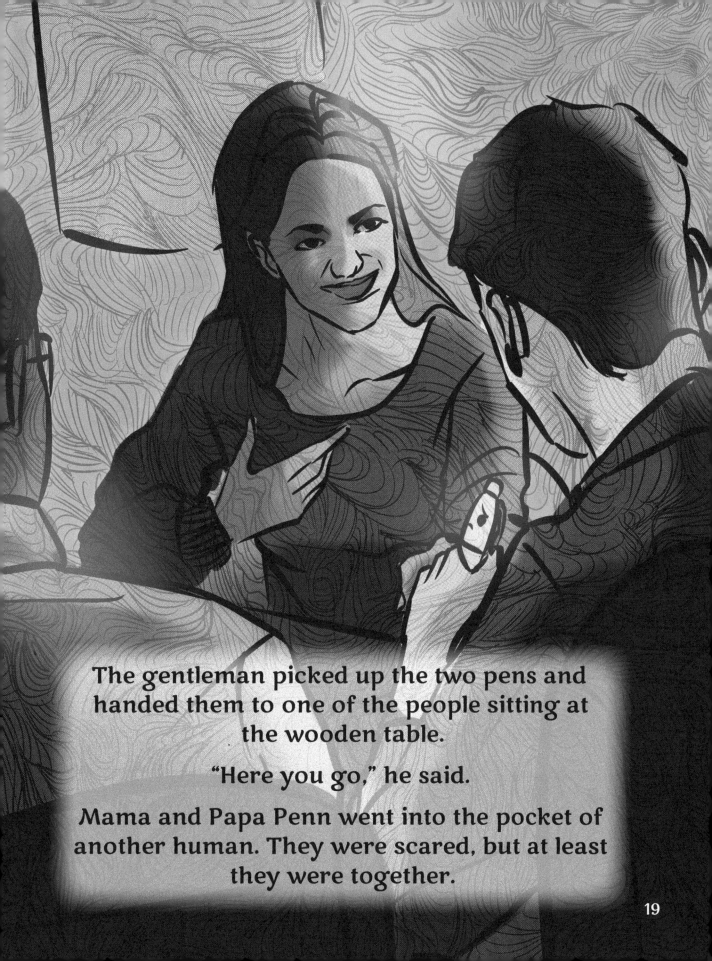

The gentleman picked up the two pens and handed them to one of the people sitting at the wooden table.

"Here you go," he said.

Mama and Papa Penn went into the pocket of another human. They were scared, but at least they were together.

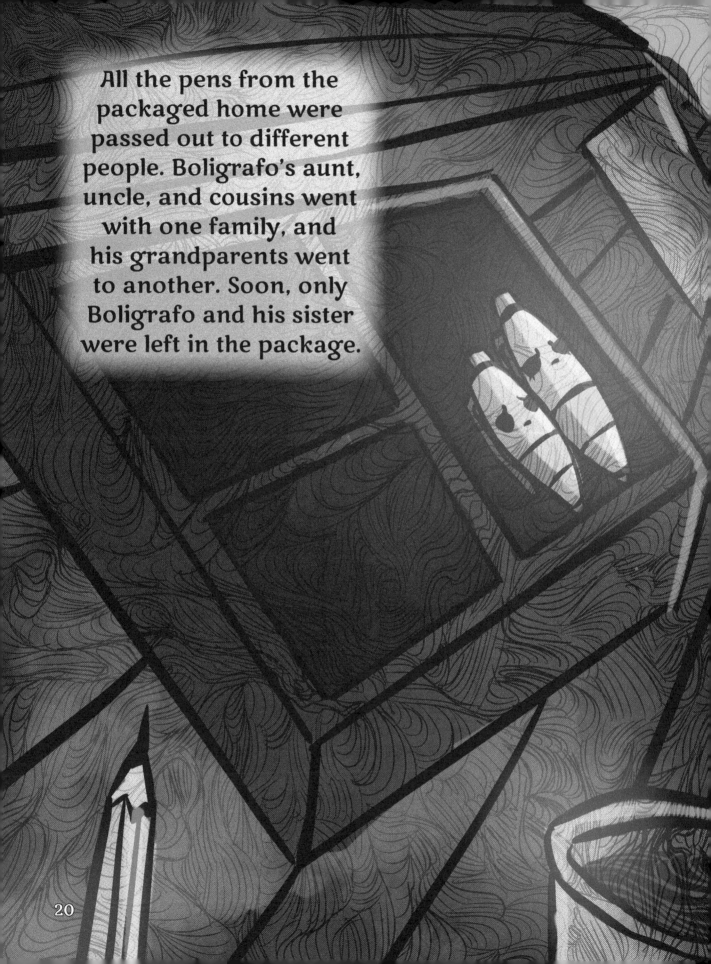

All the pens from the packaged home were passed out to different people. Boligrafo's aunt, uncle, and cousins went with one family, and his grandparents went to another. Soon, only Boligrafo and his sister were left in the package.

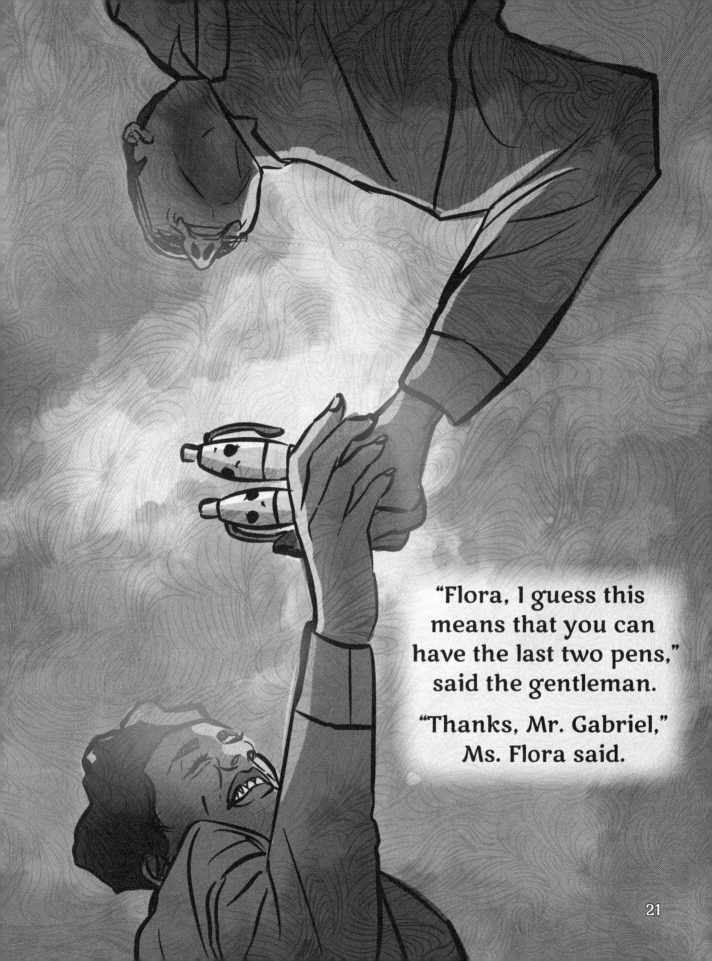

"Flora, I guess this means that you can have the last two pens," said the gentleman.

"Thanks, Mr. Gabriel," Ms. Flora said.

"Mr. Brown?" interrupted Boligrafo with the look of confusion on his face. "Are you telling me that the stranger from the grocery store and Ms. Flora know each other?"

"Well, yes, yes, they do. That stranger is Ms. Flora's boss," explained Mr. Brown.

"Oh, I get it! That means that God answered Grand Mama Penn's prayer!"

"Precisely," Mr. Brown said. "She prayed that you would be in a safe home and that you would be protected."

A lightbulb seemed to go off in Boligrafo's precious mind. "The stranger was our angel!" he exclaimed. "I thought he was there to harm us, but he did just the opposite! I miss my family, but Ms. Flora is so kind to me. She takes me everywhere she goes!"

23

"Ms. Flora is incredibly compassionate and always takes good care of those she loves, Boligrafo," Mr. Brown said, reaching over for a hug. "Now, it's getting close to bedtime, and you need to get some rest."

Boligrafo leaned in and began to drift to sleep. Before he closed his eyes, he said a little prayer.

"Dear Jesus, thank you for giving me a safe place to live where I am loved and cared for. I hope to see my family one day again, but if I don't, I know You are with them. Amen."

"Mr. Brown," Boligrafo said in a quiet voice, "thanks for sharing this with me. I always wanted to know where I came from and how I got to my new home."

26

"My pleasure," said Mr. Brown with a smile.

The End

LET US TALK ABOUT IT!

1. How many people do you live with? Who are they?

2. Mr. Brown was able to help Boligrafo by telling him where he came from. Do you know someone who can help you learn more about your family?

3. When your parents do not get along, how does that make you feel? What do they disagree on?

4. Grand Mama Penn prayed that God would keep her family safe. Is there someone in your life who makes you feel safe, like Ms. Flora?

5. Going to a new place can be scary. Why was the Penn family no longer afraid?

   Share about a time when you were afraid. Have you ever talked to Jesus about this?

About the Author

Quella C. Jackson received her bachelor's degree in Child Development and Family Living from Stephen F. Austin State University. She obtained her master's degree from Liberty University in Human Service Counseling, concentrating in parenting and child and adolescent development. She has always had a heart for children and sharing the Gospel with the world. She discovered her love for the at-risk youth at Kids Across America, a Christian sports camp, where she worked in many positions during her undergraduate studies. Quella has worked in the social services field for more than twelve years through sharing her love for Christ and serving others.

CPSIA information can be obtained
at www.ICGtesting.com
Printed in the USA
BVHW051924060721
611238BV00019B/1119

9 781662 818950